Forever Chemicals

Anne Henry

Forever Chemicals

or: The Ballad of Eric and Mina (a Modern Tale of Erotic Extremism)

Moulin & Parole

2024

M & P

Contents

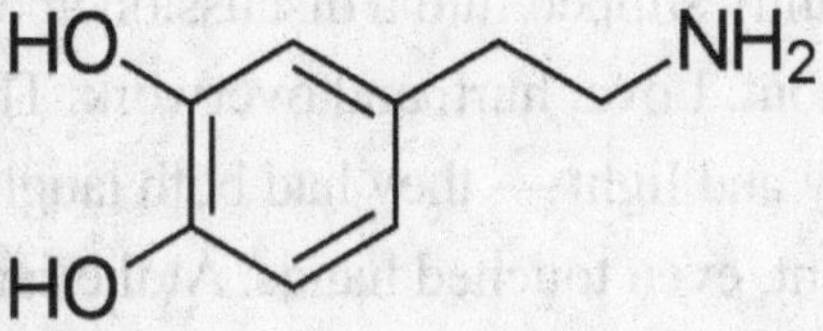

1. The Quiet Ones

Shoes on or off?

Doesn't matter, up to you, she said.

Eric hesitated, then took his sneakers off. It's impolite to track the outside in, he figured. He was a guest in this house in New Jersey — a guest of this delicately scented stranger. He wanted to make a good impression. *She smells like... herbs? Henna? What is that? God, what do I smell like. Does she like it? I hope she likes it. I mean, I'm guessing she likes it. I'm here, aren't I? In her house? Shut up, shut up, brain. Be present.* The conversation so far had been surprisingly good. He might even go so far as to say that the single hour they'd spent together — since first saying hello, in the "Lucky Dragon" cafe — had buzzed with quiet electricity. He'd ordered a cappuccino. She'd ordered a latte. He didn't eat. She ordered a muffin. They'd somehow instantly slipped into a discussion about loss, and grief, and burnout. Love, hurt, and overwork. The conversation was both heavy and light — they had both laughed and smiled and, at one point, even touched hands. At the same time, though, he couldn't quite figure out what they were doing, other than enjoying one another's company. From what he could gather, she was a chemical engineer of some repute.

*

Mina slipped her feet automatically into her house slippers. From what she could gather, he was, well, a sweet guy who lived just outside of central Philly. A grown man. But one who didn't pose much of a threat. So, yes, okay? Yes. She'd brought him straight into her apartment, this guy off the apps. She'd told him to follow her upstairs — a total stranger — after merely one hour of sipping coffee and picking distractedly at a muffin. What could she say? She was letting herself heed the tingling feeling he gave her. Oh, wait, what was his name, again? That's right: Eric. That's what he said. Eric.

The tingling seemed to happen whenever Eric looked at her — looked *into* her, she wanted to say — with his chestnut eyes under that thick dark brow of his, exuding warm curiosity.

That's what made her do it. *Come on up, Eric. I'm up this way.*

*

It's always the quiet ones, isn't it. Gotta look out for them. Mina remembered what her roommate, Alba, had told her back in chemical engineering school.

That's why I study late in the engineering department library, Alba used to say, coming home (books in arm) wearing a dirty grin. Man, in retrospect–those were the days. Alba really was an outstandingly entertaining roommate. Bless her, she did try her damnedest to initiate Mina into the ways of "empowered sluthood." Back in that era, though, Mina was only interested in long, tortured, relatively un-erotic relationships with other women. God knows why.

But Alba, for her part, well. Alba would hunt down anyone whose scent carried a whiff of sexual chemistry. *The library, I'm telling you, it's full of those ... quiet ones*, she used to proclaim, licking her finger dramatically as she flipped the page of her chemical engineering book. (She never seemed to bring them home, though. Where did they go? Just deeper into the stacks for a tryst?)

*

If Eric had heard the same warning, he would have known
better. *Gotta look out for them: the quiet ones.*

Mina was one of the quiet ones. At least, that's what you'd
gather from a first impression.

2. So, *So* "Gay"

Red-headed, and wearing a strappy, satin navy-blue day dress covered in dinosaur prints, Mina looked like she'd just stepped out of one of Eric's "hot librarian" daydreams. As she reached for the menu, her freckled arm cut a line through time and space — something straight from Martha Graham's vocabulary. Reaching forwards, Mina's breasts strained against their satin prison. Eric noticed. He hoped that Mina hadn't noticed him notice. *God, what am I, a teenager?* He berated himself, *It's cleavage, man. Just breasts. Don't be that guy.*

There was a giant black poppy flower intricately inked across her left shoulder. When she talked, her face shone. She talked openly, and laughed, and snorted, and apologized for herself. *Dang.* This woman was a *human* in a way Eric hadn't seen in years, despite working in the arts — that self-congratulating field of people who claim to know others even better than themselves. She was at home in her body in ways that even he — a tattooist by trade — couldn't fully comprehend.

You live in your skin... and you decorate your skin. And you're interested in me, a guy that doodles on people for a living. But not because of what I do or because you want inkwork for free... you actually see me for who I am.

*

She's so... sweet? He found himself saying to his work buddies, over tacos, back in Philadelphia days later. *She's kind and thoughtful and, my god, those hands. Those eyes. That brain.*

And..? they inevitably asked.

Yeah, okay, AND that rack. My god. He laughed and declined a high-five.

What else? What's she do for a living?

She's kind of a writer, he explained, knowing his friends didn't understand dating outside of the tattooing community. *She makes her living through the images in her head. And sometimes those images are of chemical compounds so small they can't even be seen.*

12

So how do you know they even exist? one of his buddies would ask.

Fuck you, he'd reply, through a mouthful of taco.

Gayyyy, they'd say, ordering another pitcher of Michelob Ultra.

No. YOU're gay, he'd retort, settling the question.

Two of these guys, in a twist of irony, actually *were* gay. But this was a way of talking they all shared together, a way of mocking actual homophobes by appropriating the use of "gay" to mean "romantic." One of these guys was probably the least romantic person you could meet. If anyone was "gay" at this bar counter, it was Eric.

Aw. *These guys*, he'd think to himself as they chortled and rolled their eyes about his speeches extolling Mina. *These guys are good guys.*

But some people just don't understand modern love. And these guys were also some of those people.

A message duly appeared in the tattoo parlor's group chat: `yo since when is Eric so friggin gay for this dyke scientist lady?`

Within seconds, the owner-manager of the parlor they all worked at — Shaun — replied with a question-mark emoji.

Ugh. *Shaun.* Eric hadn't even considered what it might be like to tell Shaun about Mina.

She's smart and funny and pretty, he thought he might say, *and we, like, connected, you know? It was electric.*

3. After The Lucky Dragon

You up this way?

Leaving the Lucky Dragon, crossing the street together, and entering her building, Eric had followed Mina's voice upstairs, up to the inside of her apartment on the third floor. It was one of those Jersey row houses where the apartment itself has two floors, and the upper floor inside the apartment is its own self-contained space. To reach it, you walk through a narrow corridor and climb up an angled staircase.

Yep! Up here. Come on up, and meet Moushi.

Wait, who's Moushi? Eric thought to himself, *I'm coming to this apartment to… meet her roommate?*

*

The room was lit indirectly, beams of light pouring through a gap in the curtains. A lamp in the corner, poised over a comfy chair surrounded by stalagmites of books. Eric tilted his head to read a title. One of the spines in the stack of tomes said: *Pigments: An Introduction to Their Physical Chemistry.* On another, it read: *Sacred Fire: A History of Sex in Ritual Religion and Human Behavior.*

A tabby cat stretched its front legs as it glanced at the intruder. *Wait, is the roommate a cat or a human? Is this Moushi? I'm just going to assume. Yeah, that's gotta be Moushi. A cat.*

I'm gonna put some music on. You like Kate Bush?

As she pulled up Spotify on her phone, the sunlight made Mina's long, wavy red hair glow like a halo.

She's… yeah, she's alright? Is she one of your favorites?

I can't get enough, honestly.

The ethereal *thwomp*s of *Running Up That Hill*'s opening started playing. *It doesn't hurt me... do you want to feel how it feels?... Do you want to feel how it feels...?*

For a while, the two sat without speaking in the twin thrifted armchairs on the upper floor of Mina's apartment, listening to Kate Bush. Mina clearly liked the finer things — just couldn't always afford them. *There's nothing better than a luxury sofa that's already been broken in,* he imagined her saying. He imagined how he'd agree. And how she'd smile. And how they might go antiquing together in a few years. *A few years, lord. Shut up,* he told himself. *You don't even know if Moushi is a human yet.* Occasionally, they glanced at each other and were respectively surprised at how shy they felt.

They admired the shapes the cat — indeed Moushi — made as she rolled around on the rug. Eventually, Eric broke the silence.

Hey, Mina, uh, can I get a glass of water? I'm really thirsty.

Mina looked at Eric and barely repressed the thought that popped into her head: was his thirst literal? Or figurative?

Yeah, sure. But Moushi just jumped on me, as you can see. So, well… There's a glass in the kitchen cupboard downstairs. Help yourself.

Eric got up and walked downstairs again. As he went, he admired the framed prints hanging on the wall: there were quite a few with poppies in them, he noticed. Unadjusted to the dim light, he blundered through the corridor, but managed to find the kitchen and turn on the faucet. She didn't seem to have a water filter. Then, without thinking, he shouted upstairs: *You need anything, babe?*

He froze. *I mean, uh, can I get you anything, uh, Mina? … Mina? … You need anything?*

Luckily, there was no reply. Apparently, she hadn't heard him.

OK, but why on earth had *THAT* come out of his mouth?!

*

She didn't hear the words he was shouting from the kitchen, over the music, but she thought his fumbling was cute. Plus, as

18

he came upstairs again and opened the skylight at her request, she got to glimpse his butt as he reached upward. He sure did fill out those boxer shorts under his jeans nicely. *Thanks ba— uh—thanks,* she said, catching herself as he undid the latch.

They had met a few weeks beforehand, on one of those online dating sites where you're asked to *trust the algorithm.* Now, she could see that Eric was that rare bird: a person who looked better in person than they did on the app.

Not that his photo gallery hadn't been attractive enough. One of the pictures looked like a professional head-shot, and the photographer had certainly done their job of making him seem capable and alluring. He had a supple, athletic build, without seeming like a gym bro. His shoulders, his hands, and his jaw all looked like they were really strong (did that make Mina shallow? She liked a strong jaw. Who can judge?). His eyes were warm and kind. He exuded humor and confidence, with only the tiniest hint of cockiness — the playful kind — off-setting his friendly, happy-to-help demeanor. His thick, dark brown hair was tied up in a little knot at the back of his head. There'd been a lovely picture of him playing with a ferret, or some such frolicking creature, looking happy as a clam. Another one had instantly given her an oddly powerful gut feeling about him, some kind of witchy feeling, she supposed, inspiring her to just go for it. She'd sent him the following message:

Hey! listen, we seem like a strong match. But I don't enjoy chit-chatting on the app. If you're interested, come and meet me for coffee at 10am on Thursday at the Lucky Dragon Cafe. I live in the apartment block opposite.

Sounds like a good time, **he'd replied**. See you then.

4. Moushi Gets Locked Out

At the Lucky Dragon, Mina had told Eric about her latest book. *I'm a scientist trying to be a publicly accessible writer,* she said, *I write about chemical engineering matters. Stuff I'm sure you'd be bored to hear about.* At this, Eric had sipped his coffee, feeling outclassed. *Well, I'm a tattoo artist,* he'd eventually replied. *I draw pictures on peoples' bodies.*

You're a tattoo artist? That's actually kind of spooky.

Why?

Mina was about to say: *Well, I've been considering saying yes to a not-particularly-lucrative development project all about the color-fastness and light-fastness of tattoo ink. So I've been reading the literature on what actually determines the longevity of subdermal inks. People have been trying to figure*

*out how to improve pigment permanence by doing nuclear
magnetic resonance spectroscopy, microwave acid digestion
and thermogravimetric analysis on various fine-particle
suspensions...*

But she thought the better of it. After all, she didn't want to
scare the man away with jargon. So, what she actually ended
up saying was this:

*Oh... Uh, just because I got a new tattoo recently. I just
adore the sensation of getting a tattoo. It's a black poppy,
see? Something that doesn't occur in nature. Poppies are
really densely full of color pigment. They're chock-full of
anthocyanins — the thing that gives fruit and veg their bright
colors. I'll shut up now. But, uh, yeah, I'm really interested in
pigments.*

While she showed Eric her shoulder, though, she smiled
inwardly at the fact that tattoos had come into her professional
life, followed by a tattooist in her personal life. And a very
charming one at that.

*

Mina had recently had a death in the family. Eric had been through a traumatic breakup. Disparate as their livelihoods might seem, they felt instantly magnetized. Clearly, they were in mourning, yet, somehow, they also knew that they could cling to one another *without* death as a pretext. A sympathetic voice. A kind ear. The kind of human touch that had been unavailable to them in the pandemic, even in the context of their pre-existing relationships — touch they needed and craved — all of this seemed to hang as a promise between Eric and Mina in the pheromone-laden air at the Lucky Dragon.

First date? Asked the barista at the Dragon, coming by to clear some plates.

I'm pretty sure we've known each other for decades, was what they both wanted to reply.

Sure, they'd each found someone with similar values. But it was more than that: it was something about the kinds of animal they each were. An unspoken, unconscious shared recognition between them, that touch is life. To connect is human. Human touch is divine.

Like I mentioned, I live just across the street, Mina said as they were standing up to leave, *want to see my place?*

*

When Eric, at Mina's apartment, excused himself to go downstairs again to use the restroom, Mina decided to do something she'd never done before. She decided to slip her knickers off from under her dress — just to see if he'd finally get the hint. *To connect is human. Human touch is divine.* She wanted that divine touch.

Re-entering the room, Eric handed Mina a can of seltzer from her fridge and sat back down on the armchair opposite her.

Refreshment for me, unsolicited. And in my own house. What a gentleman, Mina thought to herself. Moushi jumped onto the arm of her chair, as usual, to inspect the cold can.

Always inspecting, is this one, Mina sighed, giving the kitten a grin. Then she made eye-contact with Eric, patting the tabby's head while smiling — and slowly uncrossed her legs.

Eric choked on his water. Mina pretended nothing had happened.

So, Eric, do you like cats?

Every cat is different. I like your cat. It looks like this house is really set up for her.

Moushi. Her name is Moushi, remember?

Right. Good name. Yeah, it looks like Moushi really owns the place. Lots of corners to explore and places to hide and good sunny spots for naps.

Moushi skipped off Mina's lap to rub her gums on Eric's calf.

My wife and I adopted this little one a few years ago. She's so, so, so naughty. You have no idea. We love her and hate her and love how much we hate her and hate how much we love her.

Moushi jumped onto Eric's lap, standing on his thigh tentatively.

God, I really can't read signals, Eric fretted to himself. *First I'm invited over, then I'm pretty sure I just saw her labia (my god my god my god) and now, did I hear that right? She's married to a woman? And, if I'm actually right about the signals I'm picking up here, am I going to be expected to eat pussy as well as a lesbian eats pussy? Lesbians that share a cat together?*

Mina leaned in and tapped Eric's forehead. She raised a playful eyebrow. *Hey there. What are you thinking about, space cadet?*

Uh... sports. He replied, coming back to Earth.

Sports? Interesting. I totally believe you.

Eric said nothing. He was staring at Mina's mane of red hair, marveling at the way her blue eyes blazed when she flirted.

Listen, announced Mina finally. *I'd like to get a few things out of the way. From the look of your face, you didn't understand, or didn't remember, or didn't read properly — doesn't really matter which — all the things I included on my profile about "ENM" (ethical non-monogamy). So, let me refresh your memory. Louise is s my legal partner — my wife — and we've been together for 7 years. Right now, she is away for the week, on a business trip. I am totally open with her about everything, wherever we both are in the world. She and I have always been completely open, both sexually and romantically. Like, she has a girlfriend, Steph, who lives in NYC. Sometimes we all hang out as a trio. So, yeah. I want to be completely clear. Louise and I are intimate and in love. Also, we sleep in separate bedrooms. She's my nesting partner. My heart is not tied down.*

Oh. That's cool. Actually, I used to be non-monogamous by inclination. It's how I'm most comfortable — striving for non-possessiveness and transparent communication. But then, well… I ended up with someone who was kind of the opposite, unfortunately. I got into a really toxic marriage. It lasted three years and ended a year ago. I've only just recovered.

I'm very sorry to hear that. Mina stood up and grabbed Eric's hand, leading him to stand. *But I think we've talked business long enough. Come, I'd like to show you the bedroom. Come downstairs to my bedroom with me.*

Look. That one's Louise's bedroom. This one is mine.

I like it, Eric stuttered, *I like that there are…* he trailed off, not knowing why he opened his mouth. *Fabrics. These are pretty fabrics.*

By the time they had reached the end of that narrow hallway, Mina's dress had been hanging onto her body by a single shoulder strap. When she turned through the doorway, he could have *sworn* he saw a nipple. Eric's heart, for whatever reason, started pounding too hard to allow him to say anything more, so he walked straight past Mina to the bedroom window. *Nice view*, was all he could manage, as he faux-nonchalantly turned his back.

Somehow he could sense that Mina was sitting on the bed, but he didn't dare make sure.

Can I read any of your academic papers? he asked, out of nowhere.

Oh... I'm embarrassed for some people to read my work, she said.

I'm embarrassed for some people to see their own tattoos, he replied. *When you're first starting out, you do a lot of stuff you're embarrassed about. Not that — you know — not that you're just starting out, or anything... I mean–*
28

Tell me about it, she replied, *I started my career advocating for forever-chemicals. I know what it's like to leave a mark.*

Spoken like someone without a three-eyed Snoopy on their ass.

Hey, I thought I recognized you...!

Eric laughed. Mina grinned, and patted the spot next to her.

Oh... ha. Does Moushi really respond to that? Does she jump up when you pat the bed?

Eric, said Mina very slowly and deliberately. *You know it isn't Moushi I'm hoping for. In fact, what do you say we lock her out? Some things, a kitty doesn't need to see.*

And it was exactly then that Eric finally digested the invitation she'd been making to him this whole time. ...*oooOOoh*.... She *wasn't* just playing with him after all.

Wordlessly, he flashed Mina a fake military salute, ushered
Moushi out of the room, and shut the door.

I'm digging the... the chemistry, said Eric, *between you and
me. And I'd like to explore more.*

As he slid down to sit next to her on the bed, Mina smiled
coquettishly and drew her lips to his. Her mouth was startlingly
soft and tasted faintly of coffee and chocolate. Her fingers
trailed the side of his neck. He responded to her kiss, touching
the side of her face — but panicked uncharacteristically that his
fingers might be sweaty. Very gingerly, he caressed the slope
of her collarbone. She touched his arm. His hand cupped her
lower back, drawing her in.

As if by magic, every trace of his anxiety vanished. The world
closed in on them and they were the only people who had ever
existed, there in that little Jersey apartment.

5. What Happened Next

They kissed, sitting perched atop the cool duvet cover, warmed slightly by the patting of Mina's hand. She nudged towards him. He scooted even closer towards her.

And then, it all happened. There was no more trepidation. They were there, and they were there to finally *meet* one another.

Lips interlocked. Hands rifled through hair. Skin felt the warm touch of skin. Brassiere cups tumbled to the floor. Saliva migrated from mouth to mouth. Fingers intertwined.

If you're gonna fuck me, then fuck me! she moaned. *Have you got a condom on you? I've been wet basically since you said hello to me.*

Eric grabbed her by the waist and turned her onto her hands

and knees.

As he unscrolled the rubber over his absurdly intense erection, Eric quietly said: *I don't know what you are up for. I've only got one rule, I guess. I don't do anal on the first date.*

... And the second? she returned.

Eric blushed, genuinely shocked. *I mean... if you think you can fit–*

–Baby, you haven't seen anything yet.

*

They slammed down on the springy mattress. She whimpered. His cock slowly dragged against her labia. She really wasn't lying about how wet she was. Her wetness was pouring down from her, pooling on the duvet. He resisted the temptation to rub her outer labia and steal a taste from his thumb. Her pussy lips moaned themselves open. He slid inside of her.

Fuc–

Time suddenly stood still. Circlusion means *to encircle* or *to wrap*. Eric felt wholly circluded. Mina surrounded him. She engulfed him. Her wetness drew him in, panting and dazed.

It felt as though the world around them was a sea of hands pulling them in towards one another. Warm skin pressing against warm skin. Sweat mixing with sweat. Tongues. Genitals. Licking. Rubbing. Pressing.

As Eric penetrated Mina, she reached down and grabbed his shaft with her left hand, feeling it slip in and out of her body. She motioned to him to keep railing her while she worked her clitoris with her right hand. She moaned, her back arching against the bed, pointing her hard nipples upwards.

Then she wriggled free and flipped herself onto her back, spreading her legs wide and welcoming him in. Pausing only momentarily to admire the rosy appearance of her neat little carrot-topped quim and a clitoris so hard it was bursting forth from its tight hood, Eric plunged back inside her. *Some lesbian,* he found himself thinking in a fleeting instant. *Dude. This whole thing was preposterous.* This stranger was moving as though she was perfectly habituated to his body. See, the way she effortlessly returned the fingers of her left hand, from her new standpoint, to that same encircling grip at the base of his shaft that she'd been holding in doggy-style.

Feeling him move in and out of me. Feeling it with my insides, and with my fingers.

I want her to feel me pulse inside of her, he thought, *I want her to feel how good she makes me feel. I want her to feel how turned on I am as I pour myself into her. But... not yet.*

With her back to the mattress, now, Mina returned her right hand to her clitoris, too.

Only then did he notice that her belly, as she lay beneath him — her body curled up around their sticky genital point of connection — was covered in exquisite little spidery tattoos of what looked like molecule diagrams.

Serotonin? He thought, *Maybe oxytocin? Another question for another time.*

Methodically, as he rocked back and forth inside her, her

fingers worked the hood of her engorged clit, round and
around.

Fuc– she moaned.

God, baby. That feels so g–

He grunted. He could feel the internal paroxysms of her orgasm
and almost let everything go. This was dangerous territory: he
didn't want things to end so soon. He wanted to keep fucking
Mina for hours. Quickly and carefully, he pulled out as far
as he could while still feeling the warmth of her cunt on the
underside of his cock. He'd saved himself, just about. He still
felt at imminent risk of spilling over.

But then Mina whispered urgently: *I want to see you cum. I
want to see you cum.*

Eric knew it was all over for him now.

Can I take it off? she asked.

Eric nodded, and Mina's nimble fingers rolled the taut, translucent shell off his shaft. She dropped it on the floor, and cupped his balls in both hands, seemingly focusing all her attention on a drop of pre-cum he was secreting in spite of himself. Ever so slowly and deliciously, she brought the soft hot breath of her mouth to his leaking glans.

Mina looked up at him with a sudden hunger. *Eric, I know we're doing unprotected sex on a first date right now, and that was my request. So please feel free to say no. But would you feel comfortable rubbing this cock ... this magnificent cock ... um, against the outside of my cunt? I just... I just... I really, really want to see you cum all over my pubic hair. Just so you know I'm all clean. I had my last test a month ago, for STIs, and it was all clear. How about you?*

There was no time to think. Eric shuddered *YES*, and without warning, as soon the underside of his naked cock touched Mina's vulva, he erupted against her stiff clitoris and soft lips, shooting his cum across the orange pelt she kept half-secret between her legs. *Jesus.*

He collapsed to one side of her, and they lay, eyes closed, like that, for several moments.

When she thought he wasn't looking, she rubbed the cum in,
down to her skin.

*

The slightly comical reality, at that point, was that Moushi
wanted to be let back in. Her paws were even probing around
indignantly underneath the door. Somebody had to get up and
let her in. *Wait, have hours gone by, or merely minutes?*

Eric suddenly realized that he had been tracing circles on
Mina's flushed, damp collarbone with his fingers, an uncannily
intimate gesture. What was he thinking? And what was *she*
thinking? What was this? Was it too much? Whatever it was, it
felt right. But after such passion, a voice calling itself Reason
nervously piped up: *Too much too soon?*

*

Mina broke the silence as Eric let the cat back in:

*I think it's important to look at love — like, eroticism, you
know? — as something that pretty much any sentient being*

experiences. Love, like love-love, can cross species and gender and all of that. Love is an action. I love this cat. This cat sleeps on me at night. This cat has licked my blood. This cat has vomited on me. We are bound to one another.

Eric hadn't quite thought of it that way before.

*

Vertigo notwithstanding, lightness somehow prevailed. As soon as they recovered their breath, Eric and Mina started chatting again, for all the world like they'd known each other for months if not years, and hadn't just met on an app and shared an adulterous bareback fuck that made the earth move.

6. The Rest of that First Date

Mina and Eric's first date still wasn't over.

Hey, so. I'm the guest here, but… should we take a shower? Clean up? For the second round?

The second round?! Mina thought. *That was maybe the most intense sex I've ever had. A total stranger just came all over my vulva and it felt like heaven. I thought we were done for the day?*

Um, sure. She covered herself up in a throw blanket and followed him into the bathroom. Running the shower and waiting for the water to get warm, he was standing there, butt-naked and relaxed. He leaned against the sink with his hip. Against her black-and-white tiles, as he let his brown hair fall out of its hair tie, he looked right at home there. It felt uncanny.

She shrugged off the feeling of déjà vu.

So... you come here often? she asked with a comedic leer.

No, but hoping to become a regular, he gamely replied.

Mina bit her lip. She would have liked to bite his. *Are guys into having their lips bitten?*

*

Join me? Eric was beckoning her.

OK. Mina dropped the throw on the floor and stepped into her shower, an environment made all of a sudden unfamiliar by the wild, dizzy feeling this stranger created in the pit of her stomach. He soaped up a loofa and nudged her shoulders around, washing her back.

*

Why was she looking at him so intensely? Eric rubbed the sponge over Mina's body. Naked, wet, warm. Bringing her close, her breasts poured water as the stream hit her face. She gasped. He pulled her even closer, out of the way of the jet, and let her feel a heavy breath against the back of her neck. As they stood clasping each other in this way, it was impossible not to feel it. His cock grazed against her lips. Eric was already rock-hard again. Her whole body in his arms. It felt warm. Wet. Inviting.

He got to his knees, there in the shower. Water poured from her breasts, from her chin, from her pubic bone. Eric drew her vulva into his mouth, sucking her in deeply. His tongue wrapped around her clitoris, pushing her hood up and back and she moaned. After a few moments (and at least two moments of coughing and almost drowning — *at least I'd die doing what I love*, Eric thought), he stood back up.

Did he push her against the wall, at this point, or did she lean back against it? The question was immaterial. They were there–then–now. Mina arched her hips towards him and placed one foot, a little awkwardly, on the shelf where the soap was kept. She grabbed his cock and pressed it against her opening.

Wait. Wait. Sorry, wait, he said. *We can't do this without a condom. Can we?*

Maybe this will make you think less of me. But I really, really, want to, Eric.

I want to, more than anything, Mina.

Then let's.

*

She pulled his body into hers. He pressed his body against hers as far as it would go.

There was no logical or biological explanation for how good it felt to be inside her. He pulled out, momentarily scared of what he was feeling. His cock rested at her entrance. He held her face and looked into her eyes.

It's OK, she said. *Fuck me from behind again. It felt so intimate when you entered me like that before.*

She swiveled around, slippery against him. Now the cool tiles grazed her nipples. She gasped. Eric took all the credit for that one. *Thermodynamics. Not her purview,* he seemed to think. He was feeling kind of hysterical, by turns deadly serious and bubbly-silly. Jocular. Ecstatic. *Hot.*

When he came inside her, this time, it felt like coming home.

*

The strange thing was that cumming, this time, didn't do anything to diminish Eric's hardness, or his ability to keep fucking Mina: an activity he was swiftly coming to feel was his life's purpose.

Eric's cock and Mina's vagina fit together like pieces of a puzzle. Her cum mingled with his. Even under the beating of the shower-stream, he could already tell with keen sensitivity when she was about to squirt, and that it was, indeed, her squirting that was drenching his member. Their cum trailed down her leg. They continued.

Moving in and out of one another, they simply floated, suspended in a timeless weightless bubble. Moushi miaowed in vain, unheard, as they fucked in the shower until the hot water ran out. *Yikes!!* Mina yelped, leapt out from under Eric's cock, and turned the faucet off with her foot.

In the sudden chill and silence, realizing that Kate Bush was still playing upstairs, they giggled.

What the hell time do you think it is?

No idea. Listen. I feel 100% drunk right now, so I'm going to go ahead and say this: I'd love to draw on you, he said. *I'd love for my work to live on your hips forever. This moment needs to be memorialized.*

Well. Mina smiled shyly. *You've already covered me. Remember? Earlier?*

Yeah, but that got rinsed off.

We'll see. Maybe I... maybe we should get dressed.

*

They toweled off. Mina found Eric's underpants. He found her bra. They traded.

How'd this get here?! He joked, picking her undergarments up from the floor. They caught each other's gaze and laughed.

So, she remarked. *Um. What just happened? Who are you? Where have you been all my life?*

They stood looking at each other — at once slaked and shy and wanting more.

Where have you been all MY life? echoed Eric. *I guess we'll, I don't know ... see each other ... later? How to say goodbye after that?!*

They wandered downstairs, towards the front door.

Is it weird to say that I want to see you again, sometime very soon? she said.

I mean, I feel the same way... he replied. They stared at each other for a moment. Then instinct took over.

Eric pinned Mina's hands overhead, against the door-jamb. Wrist to wrist. She couldn't move, could only stare at him defiantly. He held her gaze, and to his delight, she let out an involuntary whimper. Without letting her wrists go, his other hand guided itself to her crotch. *Woah. Is this what it feels like to be a total dom? Where was this ultra-alpha energy coming from?*

Are you going to miss me? he demanded of her.

She nodded yes.

Good girl. Do you want me to cum in you one last time?

She nodded yes.

Well, aren't you going to let me in, then?

Her hands still pinioned, but balancing on one foot, Mina lifted the other leg and braced it against the wall of the corridor opposite.

His cock slid inside of her like a key into a lock, aided and abetted by the tablespoons of cum (his and hers) still dripping from her insides. Within milliseconds, Mina felt like she was fainting, falling through space, experiencing new nerve endings she'd never known, all in the shape of a big, golden O. It happened faster than either one could have expected: penetration, up to the hilt. Screams. Convulsions. Thrusting. Ejaculation.

Mina pulled her dress down. He buckled his pants, not eager to leave but looking forward to the scent of her cunt accompanying him on the drive back home.

7. Eric's Aftermath

Thus it came to pass that, a scant five hours after their coffee date had begun, the two human beings known, on a certain app, respectively, as @CirclusionEnthusiast and @Inkredible, found themselves fully dressed again at last. Smiling sheepishly, Eric and Mina stood on Mina's doormat to say goodbye.

Well, as first dates go…

…That was a hell of a first date, she said, leaning in for a kiss. *We should do it again sometime.*

So, what does that mean? he chuckled, trying his best to sound casual. *Like, we ignore each other for three days and then try to play it cool? Is that what we ought to do, to be normal?*

*I think so. Something like that. Either way, we'll be in touch —
unless I have some chemical engineering work pop up. If that
happens, it's anyone's guess.*

Mina closed the front door behind him. *The front door*, he
thought to himself in amazement, *of the home she lives in very
happily with her WIFE. Her wife and roommate who is not a
cat.*

*

Eric walked down the block.

What the fuck just happened?

*This is insane. I just got out of a relationship that nearly
destroyed me. The very last thing I wanted was to get into
another right now. It is not the time to become entangled. My
star in the tattoo industry is rising. I have places to be and
things to do! I am always out of town! And before we even get
into my schedule, my emotional availability... What about her
wife? What exactly is the situation there? Could something like*

50

this even work?

He kept clicking the "lock" button on his key fob. He had no idea where his car was.

I'm gonna have to text her tomorrow that I am not available for anything serious. I don't want to be in a relationship. If we're gonna be involved in any way she has to understand that I might, at any moment, have to be on the road. I might move to a different continent. I might never be available for future… engagements? Encounters? What do you call this? Bottom line: I can't be tied down or needed or expected to be anywhere by a girlfriend. But how in the world am I using the word 'girlfriend' in a hypothetical sense right now anyway? How is this even a question arising after ONE SINGLE CASUAL HOOK-UP? Also, what was I thinking, saying yes to having sex without a condom?

Yet, even as he berated himself, Eric felt an overpowering sense of peace creeping over him, and a complete lack of regret for the decisions he had just made in Mina's apartment.

…but my god, that sex… condom or not. Wow.

His car beeped. He was relieved he didn't need to call the dealership to get a new key made. But as he drove away from Mina's house and headed back towards Philadelphia, he found himself mentally spending his key-fob replacement money on future dates. Dates with Mina.

Hey, if I don't need to drop three hundred bucks on a new car key, maybe we could turn that into... a night in a swanky hotel? I'm sure there are some good hotels with waist-high furniture that needs exploring...

Wait! He shuddered. *I'm getting smitten. And I've been hurt before. I've barely finished being hurt. Being crushed.* (His therapist knew what he was talking about, but the reader of this novella does not. This is not to be lamented.)

Could I be in a relationship with a lesbian? A woman married to another woman?

Is it possible that marriage as an institution is problematic, and that many of your personal issues stem from an underlying assumption of the "rightness" of heteronormative, monogamistically-inclined love, versus the "wrongness" of other constellations? his therapist said from the imagined perch over the shoulder.

Yeah, doc, I hear you: it's entirely possible that this is… fine? It feels fine. It looks fine. It feels good. And that ass. My god. I've never felt so understood. Contemplating Mina's ass in reverential silence, his therapist (at least as far as Eric pictured him in that moment on his drive home) understood as well. Mina's ass, in Eric's head, wagged at him, begging him to come back. He hoped the feeling was mutual.

8. Mina's Afterglow

Mina woke up in her separate bedroom the next morning with a very wet crotch. *What kind of first date was this? One that delivers not one but THREE orgasms for the woman, from a MAN, I can't believe it.*

Louise was still away.

Also… pondered Mina to herself, *I'm confused. Can a lot of guys do that nowadays? The stamina. The railing me, rock-hard, hours on end. Have they put something in the water supply or something? Is it normal now for guys to be able to go again, immediately after cumming, straight away, three times in a row?*

But then Mina remembered Eric's face, in response to her face of surprise, every time he got hard again, or remained hard despite climaxing. She'd been able to tell that that state of affairs wasn't especially normal, even for Eric. *Hey I'm not a machine!* she could imagine him joking. *It would appear, however, that you inspire me to do great things, Mina.*

Hot and bothered beyond belief, reminiscing on all of the above, Mina pressed her Hitachi magic wand against her cunt. Fifteen minutes later, she buried her face in a pillow to muffle her screams. Screams that Eric, himself, had been imagining as he jerked his cock in the shower before work that very morning.

*

Not long after Eric left — maybe a couple of hours later — Mina had face-timed Louise to say goodnight, as it was late in Louise's work-meeting's time zone. She'd listened to her vent about her business trip's various stresses, and told her how much she loved her. *My love*, she'd then delicately said. *I know this is kind of sudden. But I went on a hook-up app yesterday and hooked up with someone. And I thought it would be nothing but the truth is, I think I might have met someone. I have to be frank with you that I actually decided to take the condom off, which I know is not exactly against our "rules," but nevertheless isn't what you'd call best practice. I hope you understand, it was a hell of a ... a connection, and I don't regret the decision. Well. It's too early to say, on that front, I guess. Maybe I dreamed the whole thing, is how it feels, a little bit. In any case we had, uh, quite a lot of sex. I just wanted you to know all of this, and I understand if you are upset, especially about the condom part.*

Louise had raised her eyebrows in response to this, listened thoughtfully, and turned up — albeit a little surprised — genuinely delighted for Mina. *My, my. That sounds kind of ... wild. No, I trust you. As you say, it's not against our agreement. And, no, my angel. Of course it's all good. I appreciate the candor and the care, though. I just think that what you got to experience sounds, well, wonderful. I can't wait to hear more when I get back on Tuesday.*

Mina had breathed a sigh of relief. Louise was rarely jealous, but — well — you never know.

Thanks, my angel. Moushi and I miss you.

And I miss you. I miss all three of my girls: you, Steph, and Moushi. And just to reassure you again: thanks for telling me. About this guy Eric. I can tell you're a bit freaked out. But I'm just really happy for you. Curious to see where things go for you two from here. Goodnight. See you in just a few days.

*

Mina grinned to herself throughout the day. She was a mess, in the best possible way. A wet and sticky mess.

Nothing stayed in focus. In the middle of stacking the dishwasher, she suddenly had a flashback from the diffuse, unending quasi-climax she and Eric had shared in her shower.

Sending work emails — to her current chemistry lab team, about whether she should say "yes" to the ink opportunity — was almost impossible because her mind kept drifting back to the feeling of Eric's lathered-up hands sliding over her hip-bones and pulling her backward onto his thick, slippery cock. A cock slippery with everything they'd been up to. Hot.

It literally *kept* happening. Midway through feeding Moushi her wet food, for example, Mina had to gasp out of nowhere because she was unexpectedly possessed by the fresh, scarcely believable memory of Eric's hands pinning her up against the doorframe and penetrating her for a third round time, using his own cum as lube. *Had that really happened? Had all that really happened just YESTERDAY?* She felt almost feverish. *Why did I remember THAT just NOW? Was it the sound of the tuna slipping from the can? (hot.)*

*

WELL. who knew you could even have sex like that on a first date, Mina marveled, late afternoon, in a text message to Francine.

Get it girl!! ok we are getting a beer tonight and you are going to explain what happened, Francine replied with characteristic decisiveness.

Even though she had been the one to reach out in hopes of a

beer with her best friend, Mina grimaced a little, imagining
what Francine was going to say when she found out it had been
a man she had hooked up with. On second thought, maybe it
had been a bad idea to text Francine.

But I always text Francine. Why would this time be different?

Francine was always supportive when Mina hooked up with
a girl. Francine — with her pet squirrel and her gap-toothed
crinkly smile and her earth-goddess-y beaded skirts — was one
of Louise and Mina's oldest friends. She knew how committed
Louise and Mina were to one another, and how good it was for
the relationship to have "people on the side."

*But was Eric someone one could have "on the side," though?
How limiting are those prepositions... "on the side." "On
the inside," maybe?* Mina caught herself thinking. *What was
Francine going to say about this non-lesbian hook-up that
wasn't even, weird as it might sound, a hook-up at all, more
like ... dare she say it? The birth of a love affair.*

Francine didn't always respect or understand the fact that
Louise and Mina didn't just have "people on the side." No.
Louise and Mina sometimes had entire parallel relationships.
Parallel partnerships. They were together, as ever, but while
being with other people at the same time. Granted, it had been
a long time since Mina had a love-relationship outside her
marriage with Louise. Shoot… did she really just think the

word "love" in relation to a person she literally just met?

*

To say that Mina was surprised at how good Eric had made her feel physically would be an understatement. How many people — how many men, especially — had a cock game like that? It wasn't cocksmanship in this case so much as cock-craftsmanship. Or, was "craft" too banal a word? What's the dividing line between arts and crafts? How many people, how many lesbians even — a sacrilegious thought! — knew how to suck on a clitoral hood like that? Or grind against a G-spot like that, responding to every contraction, every outlet of breath, as though performing a virtuosic concert performance upon a very beloved cello? Eric wondered something similar — how many lesbians could possibly know how to draw the foreskin back as they took a hard and heaving member deep into their throat? Where does learning end and intuition begin?

Or maybe it was not so much the skill that had made all the difference… maybe it was mainly a matter of chemistry. When Eric had grazed her neck with his stubble, she'd instantly flooded with endorphins. When Eric had first touched the mouth of her vagina with that swollen, round, glistening glans at the end of his long fat dick, she had seen fireworks behind her eyelids.

And let's be honest: the almost alarming girth of that penis

59

surely didn't hurt matters either (although Mina could imagine
it hurting quite a bit, were one not literally gushing, flooding
with lubrication, as she had been doing the entire time Eric had
come visiting.) *And to crown it all, he's good with his hands,*
she thought to herself, *I wonder what those hands can get up
to...*

So, yes, Mina was surprised. Then again, it wasn't as though
she, a life-long bisexual, had previously thought guys were no
good in bed at all. She wasn't at all the kind of queer woman
who talks trash about men all the time — and about straight
people — in that way that so many queer scenes love to do.
Eric had even agreed at one point in their conversation together
— *Cis guys suck in bed,* he had said, alluding to some time
spent sucking dick at a convention center sauna, in an offhand
comment at the Dragon. He'd had sex with cis men, too. *Never
again.*

(It had to be admitted that Francine, on the other hand, *was*
one of those trash-talking lesbians. Francine considered herself
proudly prejudiced against "the straights" in general and
"males" in particular. For Louise's part, although she was a
"gold star lesbian," meaning she'd never even kissed a dude,
Louise thought it was unimaginative and unprogressive to diss
hetero folks, not to mention discomfiting to bisexuals. Mina
was forever grateful for this.)

Sometimes, Mina even actively reproached friends in her

LGBTQ friend circles when they slipped into the classic "men suck" talking-points. Mina felt this whole vibe was lazy and unspecific. She didn't consider talking that way about an entire population a helpful way of addressing the all-too-real problem of gender inequality persisting in society. At the same time, Mina knew all too well what the statistics on the "orgasm gap" are in America.

95% of heterosexual men report "always or usually" climaxing — once — when sexually intimate, while only half of heterosexual women say the same. Here Mina was, happily ahead of the curve. She wept for the others.

Mina shuddered. It was almost time to go out and meet Francine for that beer.

Blessed are the bisexuals, she muttered, scratching Moushi under the chin. *Right, Moushi*?

Moushi yawned and buried her face under her paw.

*

Francine arrived a little late to the tavern, but beaming, as was her wont. Signaling to Mina, Francine headed straight to the bar for her customary prosecco. Mina was already halfway through her hazy IPA. She was staring into space contentedly when Francine called out to her. Indeed, Mina, for once in her life, was relaxed, albeit a little sore from the exertions she'd been through, pinned to the door frame especially. Life was good. In a few moments, her best friend Francine would be learning that her life-changing first-date fuck had not, in fact (for once!) been with a woman. And that would be OK. Francine would hold her hand in life, as always, and help her navigate the way ahead to a harmonious coexistence of amorous pursuits, both domestic and non-domestic.

Francine sat down. She had opted for sparkling rosé. *Hi, pumpkin!*

Hiii, Fran-bear. How are you? I just want to hear how you are. We can get to my gossip in a moment.

Oh, you know, honey: can't complain! HA-HA, just kidding. Where do I begin? Maybe I'll begin with my landlord. Did I tell you he's now refusing point-blank to keep the recycling separated?

Mina sipped her beer. She unironically loved listening to Francine's colorful summaries of her life's various battles. It came easily to her to be sincerely sympathetic. Fran-bear was a kvetcher, alright, but she was self-aware with it. Fran-bear was a mensch.

45 forty-five minutes later, it was Mina's turn.

So! Fire away, my good slut. Who was she?

He. It was a "he."

No way! A trans guy?

No. A cis guy.

A cis guy?

*A tattoo artist. Isn't that a beautiful coincidence, given how
I was contemplating saying yes to that offer from that team
working on injectable inks and colorfastness? You know, the
anthrocyanins that get me going? Anyhow, I didn't tell him that
part. I might not tell him for a while, actually. Wouldn't it be
an amazing surprise if I actually helped innovate something
that makes a difference in his art? His ... craft?* — she drifted
off, thinking about those questions from earlier – *Anyway, he's
really interesting. We fucked three times in six hours, Francine.*

Excuse me?

*I know. But it's true. We fucked for six hours and came three
times. Each. On the first date.*

OK..?

And here's the craziest part. We took the condom off, which I know is nuts. All I can say is: the trust was just all there, all at once, right away. So. Who knows if I'll ever see him again, and who knows what you think of my decision making, on that level at least. But I have to tell you, I really don't regret it. I was plateau-ing so high, and cumming so long, over and over. I felt happy and free in his arms. I saw colors. Francine, to be honest with you, I don't think I've felt anything like this in a long time. I can't stop thinking about him. It's all I could do not to text him today.

Mina. Slow down. Does Louise know?

Louise knows everything — well, she knows the gist, and she told me she wants to hear everything. She says she's deeply happy for me. She'll be back Tuesday.

Well, it is nice of Louise to say that. As your good friend, however, I can't just tell you everything's fine. You are clearly experiencing some kind of chemical derangement.

Well, and so what? What is love, if not that, anyway?

What's love? It's a second-hand emotion. Tch. Taking the condom off with a total stranger, indeed. It is my job to say to you, Mina: remember who you are.

But, Francine, that's exactly what I just did! With him. I remembered everything about myself that Louise fell in love with. This is me. It's who I am. Even if you can't support me in this, I need you to accept this about me. I love men, as well as women.

Francine did not text Mina back for the rest of the year.

9. Yes, Boss

As modern relationships go, this was one of them.

Mina and Eric texted on and off every day. Then every two or three days. Something always seemed to come up.

Are you around to get a bite on Wednesday? she'd ask.

Absolutely! he'd respond — only to write back to say *Oh shit, my boss just committed us all to overtime. I'm slammed. So sorry. Next week?*

They talked about love, about life, about the incredible fucks they'd shared together. But when Eric arrived at the parlor that week, his boss, Shaun, stopped him at the door.

*You were supposed to have another six sheets of flash art done
by now. What the hell is going on? Did you meet someone or
something?*

Eric smiled. The smile betrayed him.

What happened? Shaun demanded.

*Well, I met someone online. We had a great date. She's
busy, I'm busy... I swear, I'm working on the art you need.
Sometimes things just get kinda slow?*

I need the pages for our catalog now, Eric. Come on.

Eric slunk back to his table to start drawing. He drew flowers.
Poppies, in an O'Keeffe style.

Are you kidding? Shaun exclaimed, glancing over his shoulder,
This is just... vulgar.

Hey, human touch is divine, Eric responded.

And tattooing is about dollars and cents, he replied, *Draw me something good for once. There's a convention coming up and we need to make our mark.*

Eric rolled his eyes. Unfortunately, Shaun noticed, snapping, *Hey, do we need to have a talk? I got you this job because you showed promise. You wanted this job because you said you were interested in improving. You're good, but you're not great, kid. Anything — anything that pulls you away from your work — our studio's reputation — is a problem for me. And since it's a problem for me, it's a problem for you. I don't know what's going on in your personal life, but you need to shape up.*

Eric sighed. *Yes, boss,* he said. *Asshole,* he thought, *but I guess he has a point.*

*

Mina was antsy. It was just three weeks since Moushi had first leapt onto Eric's lap. Louise had just taken her on a lovely weekend away to the Poconos. But she hadn't heard from Eric in a few days. Work had been crazy lately, both for him (or so she assumed) and for her. She had now officially said yes to the tattoo-chemistry opportunity, signed all the documents, received her lab ID card and start date. During her weekend away, she had decided not to wait any longer, but finally to make the big reveal to Eric about the "spooky" news that she would henceforth be working on an ink for, well, *his* needle-iron, better than any ink hitherto synthesized in history. She was so excited about telling him. Where was he, anyway? It would be nice to hear from him.

Just then, Mina's phone buzzed, and her heart leapt, because she could tell straight away from the avatar that popped up on her lock-screen that it *was* Eric. She recognized that jaw. He wanted to meet somewhere as soon as possible. Hurray! A date! To hell with Francine. She was going to go on a date with Eric!

HI BABE! Yep, can do. Lucky Dragon? she texted back.

No, not the Lucky Dragon. I don't think I'll be able to bear it.

Uh. What did he mean by that? A vise-like grip started manifesting in Mina's gut.

70

OK so let's meet somewhere halfway between
us? Blue Bell?

Sounds good can we do 6pm?

See u there.

As soon as she walked into the bar she realized that Eric was
going to break things off. She could just tell: from the way he
avoided her eyes when she arrived. From the heavy energy that
enveloped her as soon as she shrugged off her jacket and joined
him, beer in hand. Mina wondered if she was going to be sick
right then and there. At least he had already bought her her
favorite beer. Plus he'd set down a glass of water for her.

Mina... I can't do this anymore. Wow. There it was. Mina
gulped her water.

I– I genuinely don't know what to say. Can you tell me why?

You're married.

Yes. I am. So?

So, you ultimately aren't available for a relationship. In society's eyes anyway. You aren't.

But, Eric, I am. I am available. We keep going over this. You're the one who keeps telling me that you're not available.

Well, I'm NOT available, actually!

Right. And may I ask, why is that?

Mainly it's that I have to focus on my work right now. I can't have anyone tying me down, because I have to be able to travel for work.

I mean... Where my career is at, I travel just as much, if not more, for work, than you do. I don't really understand. Do you want me to want you not to travel? Would it feel better if I asked you not to go places for work?

No. Yes. I don't know. The main thing, in the end, is that polyamory is just bound to be more work. It's too risky, on the one hand. And on the other, it's way, way too much work. And besides — my boss is really riding my ass right now. I'm falling behind and, yeah...

More work than monogamy? More risk than that? No, I don't think that's necessarily true at all. And, fuck your boss.

Everyone says so. Regardless, I agree with you — fuck my boss. But I have to draw dozens of images for him — to his standards — by this time next week. I'm slammed.

Yeah. A lot of people say poly is more difficult than monogamy. I happen to think they are wrong. I want to see the evidence.

The thing is, most of the people in my life would never understand or respect me if I go down this path, anyhow. I'll always be perceived as vulnerable if I go with you. Humiliated. And unsafe. And my job's already been threatened — I think about you too much as it is.

That sounds incredibly scary. I can see how big of a leap of trust it could take to view me as someone CAPABLE of commitment to you, not just in your community's eyes, but in your own.

In any case. I've just been hurt incredibly badly and this is not the right time for me to risk getting hurt again — personally or professionally. I can see the edge of the cliff and, well, and I'm scared.

OK.

OK?

OK.

I never meant to get entangled with anyone, Mina. This has all been a mistake. I'm so sorry.

I'm sad, but I'm not sorry that we met, Eric. It's been one of the best things that ever happened to me. That afternoon. Wow.

I just can't. I– no, I can't.

OK. I have to respect that. I guess there's nothing more to say, in that case. Except maybe I'll see you again some day. Bye, Eric.

Bye.

Mina stood up, put on her coat, and left. She made a point of swishing her ass as she walked out the door. She could feel the pull of Eric's eyes as they undressed her as she walked.

As she drove dejectedly back towards her apartment, Mina tried not to choke on the sobs she felt erupting from deep within herself.

What's wrong, my angel? asked Louise in concern as soon as Mina got in. *Did something happen with Eric?*

Yes. It's over between us.

No way! Why on earth?

He's not available. Or I'm not available, he thinks. I don't know. I don't really get it. Probably it's for the best. But, Lou ... I'm not ready to– I don't want to talk about it. Just hold me. Hold me. Hold me.

10. Prague

Two months passed by with zero contact between Eric and Mina, two months that felt like an aching gray cloud casting its pall over each of their lives.

Then, it was time for the "Chemistry for the Arts" convention — the one Shaun had mentioned — and, this year, it was taking place in Prague. Shaun's company was participating to showcase a new set of designs — designs that looked better as they matured and faded into the body.

Mina's new job was taking her, for different reasons, to the very same convention center in central Europe. *What do I care about the Czech Republic?*, she thought. *I'm depressed. I guess they say that sometimes the best way to get over someone is to get under someone. Maybe there'll be a cute bartender at the hotel. Who knows.*

Mina felt a bone-deep sadness that the pigment she'd hoped to reveal to Eric as a kind of gift for his artistic expression would be birthed into a world in which they were no longer in touch.

Even if he hears about the ink, she lamented to herself, *and he obviously will… at best, it will be bittersweet. On the other hand, I guess there's a chance he might be AT this conference. It looks like, alongside all the various textile people and sculpture people, there's a thousand tattoo people here.*

They didn't land on the same flight — Mina had far too many meetings with potential investors scheduled for before the conference for that — but they landed and checked in at the same hotel within hours of one another. Like ships in the night.

On Thursday morning, yawning her way through an 11:30am lecture called *Jagua Ink: a two-week tattoo*, Mina sat in the front row. *Tattoos that last a few days? What's the point?* She asked herself. *The stuff I'm working on lasts centuries, not days.*

Eric was in the same room. He could have sworn he saw a familiar red mop of hair in the front row, but told himself he was crazy. *She's a thousand miles away. She's a chemist, but why on earth would she be at a talk about tattoos? And, besides — I'm an artist whose star is meant to be rising. I travel far too much to miss Mina right now. Get your head in the game, man.*

When Mina stood to leave at the end of the talk, she spotted Eric straight away. Why did she feel so thunderstruck? After all, the thought *had* already crossed her mind that he might be in the same room. It *had*, many times, occurred to her that he might be a part of the tattoo-industry side of things here at Chemistry for the Arts, one way or another. She'd calmly tried to prepare herself for the eventuality. Nonetheless, the carpeting of the convention center swam sickeningly beneath her feet. She slipped out of the lecture-hall and made a bee-line for her hotel room.

Five hours later, Eric sat in the hotel bar trying to steel himself to meet someone to spend the night with and drown his sorrows in. But no one piqued his interest. Eventually, after his third whiskey-soda, he composed a text message:

```
Hey, Mina. I miss you. Maybe you have
blocked my number, I wouldn't be
surprised. I'm at a work thing a thousand
miles away and I wish you were here. This
```

is totally lame.

New phone, who this? typed Mina from approximately a few dozen feet above him, lying on the hotel's starch-stiff bed. She waited. Ha ha. Just kidding. Hi Eric.

oof. ok... I guess I deserved that, Eric wrote.

at least you're man enough to admit that?

Mina. please. I freaked out. I got scared. I'm sorry. I miss you.

Yeah. I know.

How are you?

Mina planned her next reply very carefully. She didn't want to give the game away entirely. Not yet. That's funny, I'm miles and miles from home right now at a work thing as well. I have a big

presentation tomorrow. Gotta go over some
things now to prepare actually. It's nice
to hear from you though. Talk soon?

Talk soon, Mina. I miss you.

Eric clicked his phone off and rolled over. He resisted the
temptation to check his phone every five minutes to see if she
had texted back to say she missed him, as well. He had to put
her out of his mind: in the morning, he was supposed to go to
some talk Shaun had pretty much ordered him to attend, called
*Modified Anthocyanins in Permanent Stasis: A Revolution
for the Tattoo Industry.* Truth be told, he didn't believe any
such "revolution" was likely or possible. He was, more than
anything, tired, jet-lagged, generally uninterested. *I'm an
illustrator, not a scientist*, he grumbled. *I could be at home
in Philly right now jerking off and feeling sorry for myself
THERE.*

*

The next morning, Mina and Eric missed each other once again
at the breakfast buffet — but as he was leaving he spotted a
coffee cup with traces of red lipstick on it and felt a tingling
intuition of a Mina-esque presence in Prague.

Shit, every little thing reminds you of her, he berated himself. *She's in New Jersey. And you've probably fucked it up forever with her, anyway. And you're a dumb idiot. On the other hand... Well. Maybe it wouldn't hurt to send her another text. It's polite to say "good morning," isn't it?*

Good morning from Central European Time. Heading off to this lecture my boss wants me to attend. I think it's actually about stuff you said you're into? pigment stuff. Anyway. Hope your day is better than mine. It's gonna be a long one.

So, Mina gulped. *He wasn't just at the convention. He was going to be AT HER TALK.*

Again, Mina had to sit down and compose her next text message carefully. For real? Maybe take notes for me, then?

You got it. How's your day going, anyway?

It's almost show time for me. Like I said,
I'm giving a big work talk about a new
thing I've been busy inventing at my new
job.

Mysterious!! Tell me about it after? Break
a leg. anyway I'll take notes on this
science talk on pigments for ya.

Badges were scanned, ushers ushed, the day's proceedings
started.

Today's first talk, boomed the moderator, *is from the folks
at Pigment-Co. They've been working with an East-Coast
botanist on naturally-occurring forever-chemicals.*

Forever chemicals, Eric thought to himself, *hmm. Where
does the oxytocin from six hours of fucking fall on that list?
Certainly makes an impression that lasts a long time.*

The interlocutor continued: *We're here to discuss the idea of a
"forever-tattoo" – something that will never fade or smear, a
pigment that actually stands the test of time. Some people say
it'll even stain your bones after you're dead. Anyway, here's Dr.*

Andromina Mayland to tell you all about it.

As far as Eric was concerned, the woman who took the stage next was a blur moving in slow-motion. Red-headed, blue-eyed, bespectacled. Eric gasped. This was *his* Mina. His *Andromina*, apparently. Fuck. This was her. Here she was. They were at the same convention. In Europe. In *Prague*. Miles and miles away from New Jersey, just like she'd said. He suddenly regretted saying to her that the conference was boring.

Mina. Mina. Mina. The sight of her instantly set his pulse racing like a runaway train. Under that blazer, he knew, was her "naturally non-occurring" black flower tattoo… along with all the other inches of her flesh he'd gotten to know just as well. Not to mention — under those capris was that juicy peach of an ass, each cheek tautly straining against the fabric. He bit his lip.

It's her. It's HER, raced Eric's brain. *She must have known. She KNEW. Right? When she texted me just a minute ago? She KNEW we were at the same conference?*

As though reading his mind, in that same moment, Mina made eye-contact with him from the lectern, and flashed him an almost imperceptible, nonetheless unmistakable, wink. *Hi there, stranger. Surprised to see me?* she seemed to say.

Eric felt like he might pass out. He tried his best to smile in her direction, what he hoped was a suave, self-composed, and warmly encouraging smile.

Mina's palms wrapped around the sides of the dais, faintly white-knuckled, crimson-tipped. Eric remembered her hands' firm grip.

Every once in a while, she began, *we chemists get to innovate something exciting and new. Something that makes an entire creative industry's head turn. Something that drives artists wild with ideas, equips them with new potential, and fires their passion. Without a doubt, the work we've been up to at Pigment-Co meets that mark.*

As Mina warmed to her theme, Eric got harder and harder. He shifted in his seat. He remembered he'd promised to take notes. He strained to pull a pen out of the front pocket of his tightening trousers.

Working to understand the structure of anthocyanins, we've figured out how to create a product that the human body radically accepts. A substance that joins the human body as though becoming part of a new whole. In chemistry, I can say with confidence that it's never before happened that an artificial oxide composition interacts with the body like our new ink does. What we've found here, as we developed this pigment, is that the living dermis receiving the tattoo here simply acts as though these foreign molecules ... belong. Like they need to be there.

Oxide composition... Eric scribbled, *living dermis...* Involuntarily, he thought about the way Mina had rubbed his semen into her pubis. *...needs to be there.*

Without further ado, ladies and gentlemen, as you know, I'm here to launch the concept for: Black Poppy. The ink they all said couldn't be achieved. The ink they called impossible. We are here to tell you today that it IS possible. In fact, we've already got a prototype. With the right investment partnerships, we're hoping to have the Black Poppy range, six pigments just as colorfast and lightfast as the best-quality dyes in the world — but literally incapable of fading — on the market by next Fall. Let me repeat that. The difference is: human skin will never blur out this pigment. It will literally never fade. We modify existing, naturally-occurring anthocyanins with a peptide chain that makes their color stay put. I have the first vial of our first color. Fittingly, we're kicking this new line off with the blackest, most colorfast ink ever to hit the market.

She presented a small vial from her jacket pocket with a
flourish. The audience applauded.

The presentation continued and Eric couldn't follow it. Too
much about peptides, too little about how the ink itself handled
in a needle. Eric did his best to copy images from the slides …
but with every gesture she made towards the projection screen,
with every tilt of her shoulder, with every lick of a finger to
turn a page in her notes… he was living inside of his memory.

Thanks for your time, Mina wrapped up. *I sincerely hope our
work at Pigment-Co gives every tattoo artist in this room …
more power to their irons in a very imminent future.* She looked
out into the audience, at Eric. Their eyes met. Eric looked
away, wiping his mouth as he pretended to cough. He was the
only tattooist in the audience who wasn't drooling over the *ink*.

11. Anointed Chemistry

As the host transitioned to the day's next presentation, Eric slipped out of the room. He had to find her.

He ran into the crowded convention center's lobby and looked around. *Damn, did I miss her?*

As he searched the room, bustling with latecomers getting their ID badges, with volunteers in neon t-shirts pointing attendees towards one lecture hall or another. He felt a tap on his shoulder.

Excuse me, sir, are you looking for something? The next talk, the one about paper recycling and extracting toner for re-use is just about to start in Hall F, if you'll just follow–

—Sorry, but I'm actually waiting for someone.

A voice nearby piped up: *Waiting for someone? I thought I heard you were leaving?*

It was Mina.

Mina!

Fancy seeing you here. Come here often?

God. She had said that to him in the bathroom at her place.

No—well—yes? I don't know. Mina, let's get out of here.

Your place or mine?

Whichever you want. I regret how everything happened. I miss you, I NEED you. Let's go?

She placed her hand in his, and they all-but-ran through the lobby, across the parking lot, and into the hotel next door.

You're staying here, too?

Ding! The elevator doors opened. As they stepped in, Eric continued: *Yeah, you know, there's a great group rate, and–*

Mina kissed him — partly because she wanted him to shut up, and partly because she wanted him. Needed him, just like he'd said about her. The kiss she received in return confirmed that the feeling was indeed mutual.

Ding! The doors opened. Mina and Eric spilled out into the hotel corridor, still embracing. A flurry of hands and lips and saliva. They hit the far wall.

Which room are you? She asked, dazed, glad they hadn't just chipped teeth.

Uh, number 423. He replied, struggling to extract the key card from his still-tightening pants.

I had no idea your name was Andromina.

Well, neither did you, presumably, know I'd come up with the best tattoo ink ever invented.

They practically fell through the door as the card opened the lock.

Two beds, Mina thought to herself, *I guess if we break one…!* She also noticed the tattooing equipment laid out on the coffee table: the coil machine, clip cords, inks, sterile gloves and needles. *And there I was thinking I'd never get to see the tools of your trade.*

Then Mina turned to look at Eric, who was looking at her with an intensity she remembered from a few weeks before. She returned his gaze, beckoning with her eyes, backing up slowly with a smile on her face. *Well, if you're going to fuck me, then fuck me.*

Eric didn't need to be asked twice.

He reached under her butt and lifted her atop the waist-high credenza. With a few flicks of the wrist, he unbuckled her trousers, pulled them to the ground, pulled the gusset of her satin panties to the side, and drew her vulva into his mouth. He completely encircled her warmth, massaging it with his tongue, teasing her with a pulsing suction.

Fuc– Mina moaned. Her leg wrapped around the back of his neck. He grabbed her thigh and pulled her pubis deeper to his jaw.

She dripped. She gushed. She saw colors — the blackest of blacks and the brightest of reds. She was experiencing the world through a single set of nerve endings. Those nerve endings listened only to the palpations of Eric's lips and tongue.

I can't–I can't — she groaned, leaning back, almost tipping the dresser over as she pressed a flat palm backwards into the wall, *Eric, I need you.*

Eric didn't stop. If anything, he only became more resolute in his intentions. *She needs to know how much I've missed her. How much I want her. If I'm bad with my words, I'll use my mouth in other ways.*

Mina, in an instant, completely let go. She melted into a puddle, she and her juices both pooling into the corner between the tabletop and the wall. When she opened her eyes, he'd swear they'd never been brighter.

Well, the chemistry in this relationship clearly hasn't changed, she sighed. *Give me a minute. Can we go to the bed? I might need to recompose myself for a minute first, but I've got some things I need to do to you. First, if you don't mind, I want to watch you stroke that gorgeous cock.*

Mina stood up and helped Eric out of those restrictive clothes. She took off her jacket and fussed with her bra. *Here, let me help with that,* he offered, undoing her clasp as smoothly and suavely as a ruddy-faced teenager. He got it on the third attempt.

What a man, Mina giggled, flopping backwards onto the bed.

Eric knelt to her side, cock in hand. Mina tapped his leg, asking for him to straddle her chest. He was happy to oblige.

When I say I want to watch you stroke that enormous hog of

yours, I mean I want front-row seats. Show me how you touch
yourself. I want to take notes.

She watched from underneath him as he straddled her ribcage,
gripped himself at the base of the shaft, and coaxed a drop of
pre-cum to the tip of his dick. A finger was ready to receive it,
drawing that lubrication underneath, to his frenulum. He then
began to stroke — delicately, in circles — the head of his cock.
He leaned back, moaning softly. Mina was transfixed.

What a show, she thought, *and it's all for me.*

It wasn't long before Mina couldn't take it any longer. Staring
at this gorgeous man, kneeling over her, rubbing himself
gently, biting his lip. *I need that. I need to taste that,* was the
only thought in her mind. She propped herself up by sliding her
elbows back. *Don't you get too carried away. I have further...*
data samples to collect.

Mina rolled Eric over onto his back, his cock bounced from
side to side as he made his landing. *Newton's First Law,* she
mused to herself, *an object in motion stays in motion until an*
outside force acts on it. Let's see what I can do.

Eric noticed Mina staring. *You good, babe?*

Yeah, I was just thinking about… you know: sports, she quipped, hands trailing down his chest as her mouth approached his rigid member.

She breathed deep and gazed worshipfully at the staff in her hands. She licked him from the base to the tip. *The opening salvo,* as she once heard someone describe it, *when you start by licking it all, you let him know you're going to end by licking it all.* She then pushed a couple of fingers gently into the softness of his ball sac and began to massage the nerves underneath, through the skin. Her other hand started to work his shaft rhythmically, while she kissed and swirled her tongue over his opening.

OH GOD, said Eric, invoking some deity he didn't otherwise believe in. *Have mercy on me.*

Mina declined the plea. She instead looked Eric straight in the eye while she loosened the muscles at the back of her mouth, only to plunge him very, very slowly past the threshold of her throat. Eric felt like his whole being had become a murmuration of swallows wheeling in the summer sky; or a hard-boiled egg slipping cleanly and neatly out of its shell, shiny and new.

Mina began to taste the salt of Eric's pleasure leaking into her mouth. Her jaw began to ache from the task of circluding Eric's cock, moving up and down it with her lips, her two hands, and all the muscles of the inside of her face. At the same time, she felt like she could suck this cock all day. Nothing could possibly be a better use of her time.

You are killing me, baby, whimpered Eric, thrashing around on the pillow. Mina, her mouth being full, could only reply with an expressively fiendish narrowing of her eyes from down where she crouched.

As Mina's tongue, fingers and lips intensified their skillful, methodical torments of Eric's cock, the capillaries began to tighten. Eventually, they felt, to Mina, as though they were fit to burst.

With her eyes, she asked Eric: *Are you going to feed me your creamy, thick cum, now lover?*

With his moaning body, Eric answered in four prodigious bursts: *yes. Yes. Oh GOD, yes.*

As soon as the convulsions attenuated, Mina showed him her tongue, laden with seed. Then she swallowed, and licked her lips.

*

They weren't sure when they fell asleep, but they woke up slowly, a tangle of limbs tied together in a sweaty duvet. Eric was tracing circles on Mina's hip. She nudged herself back into him, pressing her ass into his crotch.

Morning, she said.

Is it? He replied.

Haha, I'm not sure. Hmm. No — the clock says it's two a.m.; look — it's dark outside.

Fuck, I'm flying out at ten.

In the morning?

I think so.

Don't worry, then. We've got time.

*It feels like we have all the time in the world. We're going home
to more or less the same place, aren't we...?*

*We are. And if it's the 10 AM flight to Newark, I think we might
even be on the same flight. Maybe we can get them to let us
sit together. Then we could ... you know... hold hands on the
flight.*

They lay in silence for a moment, smiling, flooded with
happiness at the prospect.

*This might scare you, Mina, but I have to say it: I already feel
like I can't imagine what life would be like without you.*

She was silent.

He got scared, and decided to ask her straight up. *Fuck it: I'm sure it's obvious but you need to hear it. I'm crazy about you. Do you... do you... Mina, do you think you might have feelings for me, too?*

Of course I do.

Eric's chest expanded all at once, like a time-lapsed image of a flower spreading under the sun.

I've had feelings for you, I think, since we stepped out of the shower at my house together.

Eric wanted to sob but instead he gave her a squeeze, palm on her chest — his hand vibrating with her heartbeat, nestled between her pert breasts. He drew her into the little-spoon position to his big-spoon, locking her tenderly in a tight embrace. His breath tantalized the nape of her neck. They breathed together, perfectly in sync.

GAY, she said, suddenly, out of nowhere. He burst out laughing. So, she liked to use that word the same way.

Then, slowly, almost imperceptibly, involuntarily, she ground her buttocks back into him. Then, at one point, it became impossible to ignore: she could feel his cock growing between her cheeks. She got wet, yet again.

I have an idea, she said.

What's that? He asked.

Well it is *the second date, isn't it?* she intoned a grin. Eric had no idea what she was talking about.

Then it dawned on him. *No anal on the first date*, he'd told her.

Eric paused, thought about it, and then deliberately moved his hand from her sternum to her crotch, grazing against her clitoris. She moaned softly, pressing back even harder into him.

Now she made things perfectly plain: *I want you in my ass so badly, Eric. I just know it will make me cum so hard. I just know it will feel so good. Are you up for it? Obviously, it's got to be gentle, okay?*

Oh, darling. I'd love to, Eric smiled. *How do you want to be? Hands and knees? On your back? Let's work up to that.*

Eric stacked up some pillow for Mina, who got on her hands and knees, propped up and well-supported, with her ass high in the air.

Eric fumbled around, thinking how best to proceed. He had his ointments in his tattoo kit with him — as ever — but he didn't have any other lubricant. He fretted for a moment, then figured that pussy-juice would have to do, and got to work.

His hands wrapped around her ass, meeting at her sacrum. He leaned in, inhaling her pussy. His tongue glanced between her labia and her clitoris, meeting the edge of her earthy, puckered hole. She gasped.

After a few moments of this, his hands slipped towards her vulva and guided themselves inside of her lips. Meanwhile, his mouth shifted all its attention towards her ass.

He ran the rough of his tongue across her opening, depositing more and more spit with every stroke. His right hand was still inside her, but now he extricated his left thumb and pressed it against her sphincter.

God, babe, just like that.

Eric smiled. He could feel her pussy gush as her ass welcomed his thumb. Within a minute, he just… slipped in. She moaned. He pressed down, ever so slightly, giving her a sense of fullness. Her hips met his pressure, amplifying it. Her shoulders slumped further into the mattress.

Working her pelvis with two hands, Eric watched Mina's stress melt away. Gone was the convention. Gone were his worries. There they were, two humans, buried inside of one another. Mina bucked against his hands. He started moving a little faster.

Fuck, fuck, fuc– Mina moaned, clinching herself around Eric's hands. *Eric, I need you. I need you inside of me right now… please…*

Eric slowly removed his thumb, still firmly massaging Mina's cunt. He got higher on his knees and guided the head of his cock towards her beckoning ass. He covered his hand in her juices, and gave himself a generous stroke with her stickiness, ensuring a smooth entry to her body, thanks to her own cum. He gently pressed his member against the little starfish between her cheeks.

They both moaned slightly. They stayed perfectly still at first, each of them incrementally adding a little more pressure against the other. Slowly, surely, her tightness gave way and he slid a third of the way in.

—AGH—just a second, Mina groaned sharply as she gripped the duvet cover tight. White knuckles and red fingertips.

Just let me know, baby. Eric held still, keeping his cock right where it was. After a deep exhale, and a count of thirty, Mina swallowed him whole.

Out of care and solicitude, though she now began to really throw her hips back, he continued to go very, very slow. If there were a record for the slowest, gentlest, and somehow most animalistic sex, this fuck would have been a contender.

But Mina let him know it was time to shift gears. *I'm ready for my railing now. Will you give it to me?*

Eric grabbed Mina's shoulders from under her arms, pulling her upright and into him. She clinched around him, moaning softly as she took his cock to the hilt.

They rolled over, his cock still deep in her ass, placing her on top. Eric's fingers gently tapped against her clit. With his hands pushing and pulling her onto himself, she rode him, bucking her hips into his, gripping him as though to force him to cum.

She started panting. Her eyes rolled upwards. Eric could feel her pelvic walls swell just before she let go completely.

Eric — I love you. Keep fucking me. Fuck me forever. You make me feel–fee–so–so–goo–

She erupted. Her pussy dripped down to his shaft, to his balls. Her back broke into a cold sweat. She thrashed before going almost completely limp — one hand desperately grasping behind herself, flailing at the side of his face. *Baby–*

Baby...

Baby I love you. Never let go.

Baby, I never will.

She sighed and fell into his chest. He received her in a warm embrace. His cock throbbed. She responded with a squeeze of her butt. That squeeze ended it for Eric. He exploded deep inside of Mina.

*

By degrees, Eric grew flaccid enough to slip comfortably out. Mina appeared to have passed out into a deep slumber, so he eased himself out from underneath her by tilting her gingerly onto her side. He tiptoed towards the shower to wash. There was surprisingly little to clean up.

Mina's breathing stayed soft and regular. It sounded somehow like the most familiar and comforting sound in the world.

Padding back to the bed, he checked the clock. Quarter to four

in the morning. He set an alarm for 6am, and slid himself back
under the sheets.

*

At 6am, Eric's alarm jolted the pair into consciousness, where
they realized with bemusement that they'd somehow become
even more entangled in each other's bodies while they slept. A
scant 2 hours of sleep.

Shit, croaked Mina groggily, sitting bolt upright. *We should
do online check-in for our flight right now, pack up our stuff,
and jump in a cab at 7 at the latest. I'm pulling up the check-in
now.*

Mhmmf, agreed Eric reluctantly, still refusing for the time being
to open his eyes.

NO WAY, exclaimed Mina. *It's delayed! Our flight's delayed.
Well. I should let Louise know. Wow. OK. Well. We can go back
to sleep. Dang. I don't think I've ever been glad before, to learn
that a flight is delayed by an "estimated six hours."*

She sent a quick text to her beloved wife, then collapsed
backwards into Eric's arms.

*

At half past 7 — the sunlight, streaming through the curtains
they'd omitted to draw — roused them again, more gently this
time.

Morning, said Eric. *Have I told you this before? Your tattoos
are gorgeous.* His eyes felt like they were gorging themselves,
studying Mina's body by the light of the dawn, admiring the
atlas of chemical compounds inscribed on the skin of her hips
and her stomach. They seemed to come alive in the glow of the
morning. *You give me so many ideas. Could I possibly — um
can I draw on you?*

Of course.

She thought to herself: *how intimate.*

He found a ball-point pen in the drawer of the bedside table,
next to the room service menu and a Kralice Bible.

Though Eric hadn't understood much of Mina's lecture, he
was good at remembering shapes and figures. He seized upon
her abdomen and started sketching out her modification of
the anthocyanin compound. *Let's see,* he mumbled to himself,
*three hexagons, two together with a line extending out to the
third...* Mina raised an eyebrow. Eric was getting this right. She
tried not to blush. *More lines coming from a few of the sides...
what were those labeled?*

R, she said, *that means "rest of molecule."*

So the compound starts from this center and then goes...

...it can be whatever you want it to be. That's the magic.

So what are the rest of these diagrams on you? They're lovely.

*Thanks. They're my life's work. Every time I create something
new, I like to get it charted across my body. Added into my
body. It's a bit of a ritual. A commemoration.*

Well, here you go. There's the latest! Eric smiled, admiring his lines.

Cool. I like it. Actually, though ... Mina flashed a self-doubting grin. (*Was this insane to think about?* she asked herself. Well, yes, it probably was insane. And she didn't care.) *I was actually already wondering whether you might do it for me for real... you see, I have that sample of Black Poppy with me, in my jacket pocket. And, obviously, you have your iron with you here. And you clearly know what you're doing... and this seems—*

—This seems like a moment to commemorate. I agree. Eric got up and plugged in his machine.

He washed his hands and put on some rubber gloves. With some alcohol and a wad of cotton, he disinfected the area of Mina's skin he'd scribbled upon. The ink from the ball-point pen came off entirely as he rubbed. He would re-do the modified anthocyanin molecule she had synthesized *free-hand*.

You're sure about this, right?

I'm sure. I want this. I want to do this now, before we catch our flight and go home.

Let me have the sample, then. She dug the small vial of jet liquid out and handed it to him. He held it up to the light, and watched it slosh around like a molten black hole. It reminded him of the new acrylic that boasted 99.4% light absorption. He selected a fine round-liner needle, and poured a small amount of the precious Black Poppy into one of his plastic wells. He adjusted his iron's grip and dipped his tip in, turning on his machine.

You ready? This is going to hurt. But you know that.

I'm ready.

His needle hovered over her, then plunged through her epidermis. She yelped, then gritted her teeth, and finally beamed. With utmost care, he began re-tracing from memory the lines he'd drawn on Mina's belly just moments before, making an indelible mark on Mina's skin. This was *her* pigment. This was *her* invention. She'd been the *first* to crack the code and enjoy the result. A result — an achievement — that would never wash away or fade with time. And he was the first to use the tools she'd provided — pigments she'd brought into the world.

"R" stands for "rest of molecule," murmured Eric as he finished the final serif, *and it means that anything can happen. It's just gotta start somewhere.*

He sat back and admired Mina. He admired his work, seeing how it fit into her existing constellations.

This will be there forever.

Some say it's already stained my bones.

*